D1442023

HANNAH SPARKLES

HOORAY FOR THE
FIRST DAY OF SCHOOL!

WITHDRAWN

By
Robin Mellom

Illustrated by
Vanessa Brantley-Newton

HARPER
An Imprint of HarperCollinsPublishers

For the students in room R-6—R.M.

This book is dedicated to every
child, with love—Ms. V

Hannah Sparkles: Hooray for the First Day of School!
Text copyright © 2019 by Robin Mellom
Illustrations copyright © 2019 by Vanessa Brantley-Newton
All rights reserved. Manufactured in China.
No part of this book may be used or reproduced in any manner whatsoever without written permission
except in the case of brief quotations embodied in critical articles and reviews. For information address
HarperCollins Children's Books, a division of HarperCollins Publishers, 195 Broadway, New York, NY 10007.
www.harpercollinschildrens.com

ISBN 978-0-06-232234-0

The artwork for this book was created by hand sketching, Photoshop, and Corel Painter 12.
Typography by Whitney Manger and Erica De Chavez
19 20 21 22 23 SCP 10 9 8 7 6 5 4 3 2 1

First Edition

I'm Hannah Sparkles. People say I can make friends with *anybody*.

I say they're right!

I'm great at giving
HUGS.

Watch this!

The more
GLITTER,
the better!

BUTTERFLIES
make everyone happy!

I'm a friend-making machine.

That's why I couldn't wait for the first day of school.
First grade would be the perfect place to make friends!

I imagined it like this: side by side with my best friend, Sunny Everbright, laughing and working. All while we met new friends. . . .

The next morning, Sunny and I stepped
up to the door of our new classroom.
We gasped.

It was so colorful.
And there were soon-to-be
new friends everywhere!

The teacher showed us to our seats.

Just before class started, I wiggled
with excitement. I was SO prepared!

Sunny was on
the opposite side
of the room.

I whispered Sunny's name.

She didn't hear me.

I waved at Sunny.

She didn't see me.

My best friend was not at my side. But that was okay. There were lots of new friends to be made. And I was prepared!

"Hi, I'm Hannah. I have the best GLITTER pens!"

"Oh."

"Like my BUTTERFLY NET?"

YAWN

I decided to crank up the charm. . . .

"Someone needs a HUG!"

"You could use a CHEER!"

"Only use the FINEST colored pencils!"

Charm wasn't working. Maybe they just needed to know more about me.

"Hi, I'm Hannah Sparkles. My hobbies are picking daisies, cheering, drawing pictures, and catching—"

"SHHH!"

Charm didn't work.
Talking about myself didn't work, either.

Nothing worked.

At recess, I rushed over to Sunny.
"No one wants to be friends with me. What am I doing wrong? I showed them my neat school supplies. And I talked about the things I love."

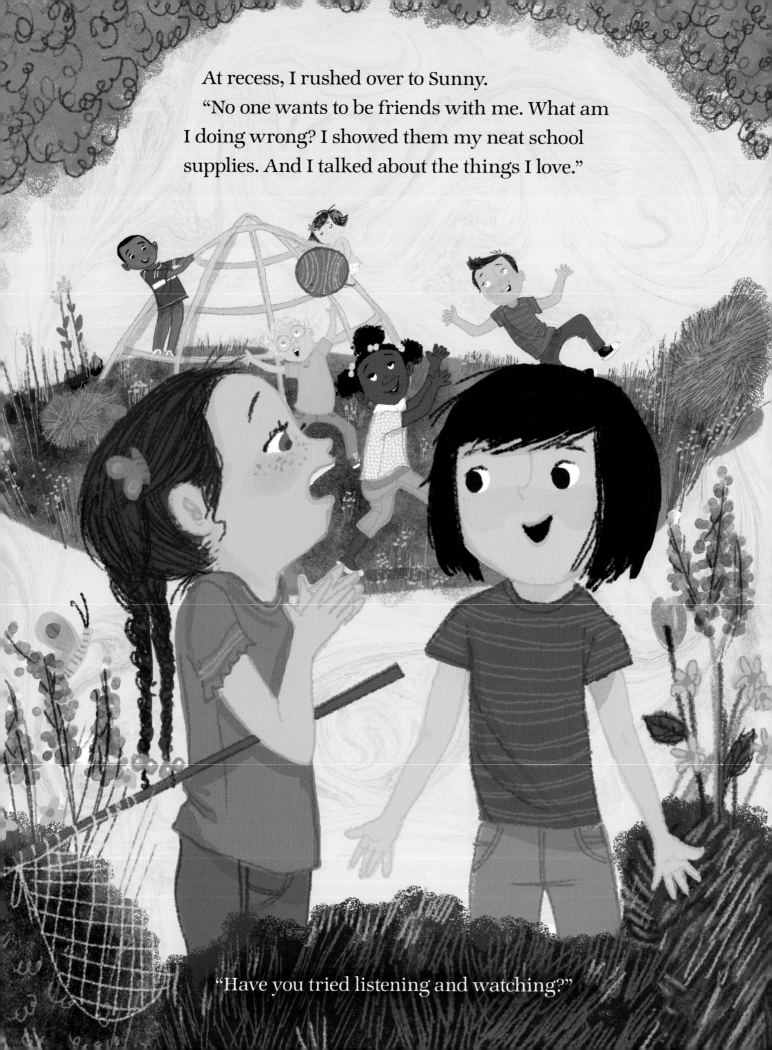

"Have you tried listening and watching?"

I gave this some thought. Listening?
WATCHING? Maybe it could work. Sunny
is so smart. "How do you know that?"

"That's what it says on your butterfly net."

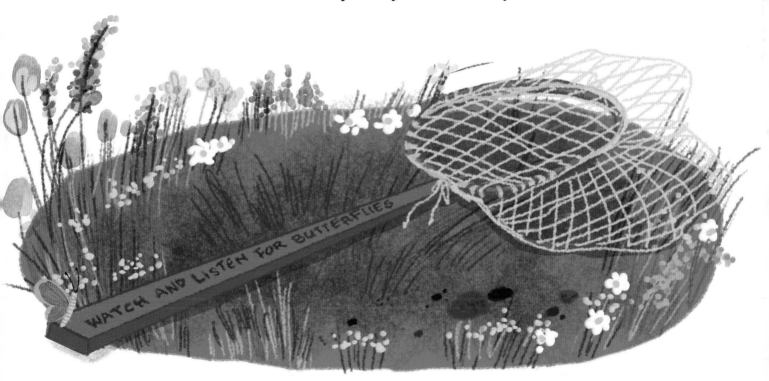

WATCH AND LISTEN FOR BUTTERFLIES

If it works for butterflies, it might work for people, too!

I tried listening. I really did. But I couldn't keep my thoughts to myself.

"Daisies. Daisies are the best flower!"

Then I tried watching. I really, really did.

Except I'm much better at DOING.

It wasn't long before the teacher noticed
me. My sad face was hard to miss.

"Need help, Hannah?"

"Everyone says I'm the type of girl who can make
friends with *anybody*. But now I'm not so sure."

"How about some quiet thinking time? This is our 'refill station.'"

"Refill?"

"Sit. Think. Refill. Then come try again!"

Without anyone to talk to, it was quiet.

Really quiet.

Then came a sound. And another one. And even more sounds. They were BEAUTIFUL sounds.

A breeze SWIRLED.

Birds CHIRPED.

Butterfly wings
FLUTTERED!

REFill
Statio

I watched.
I listened.
And . . .

I LOVED IT!

That refill station worked. I was ready to give it another try with my soon-to-be friends.

This time I didn't show and talk.
I watched and listened.

"I love their colors!"

"I can hear their
wings fluttering!"

"Aren't butterflies the best?"

"YES!"

The day ended up better
than I ever imagined.

And I imagined

A LOT!

HOORAY

for the first day of school!

31901065347413